SEDUCERS IN ECUADOR

By V. SACKVILLE-WEST

Seducers in Ecuador
Grey Wethers
The Heir and other Stories
Challenge
Heritage
Knole and the Sackvilles

NEW YORK:
GEORGE H. DORAN COMPANY

SEDUCERS
IN ECUADOR

BY

V. SACKVILLE-WEST

NEW YORK

GEORGE H. DORAN COMPANY

To
VIRGINIA WOLF

SEDUCERS IN ECUADOR

SEDUCERS
IN ECUADOR

It was in Egypt that Arthur Lomax contracted the habit which, after a pleasantly varied career, brought him finally to the scaffold.

In Egypt most tourists wear blue spectacles. Arthur Lomax followed this prudent if unbecoming fashion. In the company of three people he scarcely knew, but into whose intimacy he had been forced by the exigencies of yachting; straddling his long legs across a donkey; attired in a suit of white ducks, a solar topee on his head, his blue spectacles on his nose, he contemplated the Sphinx. But Lomax was less interested in the Sphinx than in the phenomenon produced by the wearing of those coloured glasses. In fact, he had already dismissed the Sphinx as a most overrated object, which, deprived of the snobbishness of legend to help it out, would have little chance of luring the traveller over fifteen hundred miles of land and sea to Egypt. But, as so often happens, although disappointed in one quarter he had been richly and unexpectedly rewarded in another. The world was changed for him, and, had he but known it, the whole of his future altered, by those two circles of blue glass. Unfortunately one does not recognise the turning-point of one's future until one's future has become one's past.

Whether he pushed the glasses up on to his forehead, and looked out from underneath them, or slid them down to the tip of his nose, and looked out above them, he confronted unaided the too realistic glare of the Egyptian sun. When, however, he readjusted them to the place where they were intended to be worn, he immediately re-entered the curious world so recently become his own. It was more than curious; it was magical. A thick green light shrouded everything, the sort of light that might be the forerunner of some undreamed-of storm, or hang between a dying sun and a dead world. He wondered at the poverty of the common imagination, which degraded blue glasses into a prosaic, even a comic, thing. He resolved, however, not to initiate a soul into his discovery. To those blessed with perception, let perception remain sacred, but let the obtuse dwell for ever in their darkness.

But for Bellamy, Lomax would not have been in Egypt at all. Bellamy owned the yacht. A tall, cadaverous man, with a dark skin, white hair, and pale blue eyes, he belonged to Lomax's club. They had never taken any notice of one another beyond a nod. Then one evening Bellamy, sitting next to Lomax at dinner, mentioned that he was sailing next day for Egypt. He was greatly put out because his third guest, a man, had failed him. "Family ties," he grumbled; and then, to Lomax, "somehow you don't look as though you had any." "I haven't," said Lomax. "Lucky man," grumbled Bellamy. "No," said Lomax, "not so much lucky as wise. A man isn't born with wife and children, and if he acquires them he has only himself to blame." This appeared to amuse Bellamy, especially coming from Lomax, who was habitually taciturn, and he said, "That being so, you'd better come along to Egypt to-morrow." "Thanks," said Lomax, "I will."

This trip would serve to pass the time. A yachting trip was a pleasant, civilised thing to undertake, and Lomax appreciated pleasant, civilised things. He had very little use for the conspicuous or the arresting. Such inclinations as he had towards the finer gestures—and it is not to be denied that such inclinations were latent in him—had been judiciously repressed, until Lomax could congratulate himself on having achieved the comfortable ideal of all true Englishmen. From this trip, then, he antici- pated nothing but six or seven agreeable weeks of sight-seeing in company as civil- ised as his own. It is, however, the purpose of this story to demonstrate the danger of becoming involved in the lives of others without having previously tested the harm- lessness of those others, and the danger above all of contracting in middle-age a new habit liable to release those lions of folly which prowl about our depths, and which it is the duty of every citizen to keep securely caged.

Of course one cannot blame Lomax. He knew nothing of Bellamy, and for Miss Whitaker his original feeling was one of purely chivalrous compassion. Besides, it

must be remembered that under the new influence of his spectacles he was living in a
condition of ecstasy—a breathless condition,
in which he was hurried along by his in-
stincts, and precipitated into compromising
himself before he had had time to remove
his spectacles and consult his reason. Indeed, with a rapidity that he was never well
able to understand, he found himself in such
a position that he no longer dared to remove
his spectacles at all; he could not face a
return to the daylight mood; realism was no
longer for him. And the spectacles, having
once made him their slave, served him well.
They altered the world in the most extraordinary way. The general light was green
instead of yellow, the sky and the desert
both turned green, reds became purple,
greens were almost black. It produced an
effect of stillness, everything seemed muf-
fled. The noises of the world lost their
significance. Everything became at once in-

14

tensified and remote. Lomax found it decidedly more interesting than the sights of Egypt. The sights of Egypt were a fact, having a material reality, but here was a phenomenon that presented life under a new aspect. Lomax knew well enough that to present life under a new aspect is the beginning and probably also the end of genius; it is therefore no wonder that his discovery produced in him so profound and sensational an excitement. His companions thought him silent; they thought him even a little dull. But they were by that time accustomed to his silence; they no longer regarded him as a possible stimulant; they regarded him merely as a fixture—uncommunicative, but emanating an agreeable if undefined sense of security. Although they could not expect to be amused by him, in each one of them dwelt an unphrased conviction that Lomax was a man to be depended upon in the event of trouble. The extent to which

15

he could be depended upon they had yet to learn.

It is now time to be a little more explicit on the question of the companions of Lomax.

Perhaps Miss Whitaker deserves precedence, since it was she, after all, who married Lomax.

And perhaps Bellamy should come next, since it was he, after all, for whose murder Lomax was hanged.

And perhaps Artivale should come third, since it was to him, after all, that Lomax bequeathed his, that is to say Bellamy's, fortune.

The practised reader will have observed by now that the element of surprise is not to be looked for in this story.

"Lord Carnarvon would be alive to-day if he had not interfered with the Tomb," said Miss Whitaker to Lomax.

Lomax, lying in a deck-chair in the verandah of their hotel, expressed dissent.

16

"I *know* it," said Miss Whitaker with extreme simplicity.

"Now how do you know it?" said Lomax, bored.

But Miss Whitaker never condescended to the direct explanation. She preferred to suggest reserves of information too recondite to be imparted. She had, too, that peculiarly irritating habit of a constant and oblique reference to absent friends, which makes present company feel excluded, insignificant, unadventurous and contemptible. "*You and I* would never agree on those questions," she replied on this occasion.

Lomax asked her once where she lived in London. She looked at him mistrustfully, like a little brown animal that fears to be enticed into a trap, and replied that she was to be found at a variety of addresses. "Not that *you'd* find me there," she added, with a laugh. Lomax knew that she did not mean to be rude, but only interesting. He was

17

not interested; not interested enough even to ask Bellamy. Bellamy, now, interested him a great deal, though he would always have waited for Bellamy to take the first step towards a closer intimacy. Bellamy, however, showed no disposition to take it. He was civil and hospitable to his guests, but as aloof as a peak. Lomax knew him to be very rich and very delicate, and that was about the sum of his knowledge. Bellamy's reticence made his confidences, when they did finally come, all the more surprising.

Artivale, the fourth member of the party, was on the contrary as expansive as he well could be. He was a dark, slim, poor, untidy young scientist, consumed by a burning zest for life and his profession. His youth, his zeal, and his ability were his outstanding characteristics. Bellamy in his discreet way would smile at his exuberance, but everybody liked Artivale except Miss Whitaker, who said he was a bounder. Miss Whitaker

impending disaster? So, at will, was it with
Lomax. But Miss Whitaker, for once, was
a natural woman.

"Oh," she said, looking up at last,
"do for goodness' sake take off those horrid
spectacles."

Lomax realised then the gulf between
himself, dwelling in his strange world, and
the rest of mankind in a wholesome day.
But he knew that if he took them off,
Miss Whitaker would immediately become
intolerable.

"The glare hurts my eyes," he said. So
do we lie. Miss Whitaker little knew what
she gained. Looking at Lomax, she saw
a man made absurd. Looking at Miss
Whitaker, Lomax saw a woman in distress.
All womanhood in distress; all womanhood
pressed by catastrophe. His common sense
was divinely in abeyance; and he kept it
there. What else, indeed, was worth while?

To Miss Whitaker, too, was communi-

23

cated a certain imminence. Her own stories were marvellously coming true. Indeed, to her, they were always true; what else was worth while? But that the truth of fact should corroborate the truth of imagination! Her heart beat. She kept her eyes averted from Lomax; it was her only chance. He kept his eyes bent upon her; it was his. At all costs she must not see the glasses, and at all costs he must see through them, and through them alone. He gazed. The chair she sat in was a smoky cloud; her fragility was duskily tinged. Her tears were Ethiopian jewels; black pearls; grief in mourning. Yet Lomax had been, once, an ordinary man, getting through life; not more cynical than most. An ordinary man, with nothing in the world to keep him busy. Perhaps that had been his trouble. Anyway, that was, now, extravagantly remedied.

It took a long time to get a confession out of Miss Whitaker. She could write Ecuador

on an envelope, and without comment allow
it to be observed, but she could not bring
herself to utter so precise a geographical
statement. There were moments when it
seemed to Lomax, even behind the black
glasses, perfectly ridiculous that he should
suggest marriage to Miss Whitaker. He did
not even know her; but then, certainly, the
idea of marriage with a woman one did not
know had always appeared to him a degree
less grotesque than the reverse. The only
woman in his life being inaccessible, one
reason for marriage with anybody else was
as good as another. And what better reason
than that one had found a lonely woman
in tears, and had looked on her through
coloured glasses?

Miss Whitaker knew only that she must
keep her head. She had not thought that
the loose strands cast by her about Lomax
could have hardened so suddenly into a knot.
She had never known them so harden be-

fore. But what an extraordinary man!
Having spent her life in the hopes of coming across somebody who would play up, she
was astonished now that she had found him.
He was too good to be believed in. Very
rapidly—for he was pressing her—she must
make up her mind. The situation could not
be allowed to fritter out into the commonplace. It did not occur to her that the truth
was as likely to increase his attention as any
fiction. She was not alone in this; for who
stands back to perceive the pattern made by
their own lives? They plaster on every sort
of colour, which in due time flakes off and
discovers the design beneath. Miss Whitaker only plastered her colour a little thicker
than most. She was finding, however,
that Lomax had got hold of her paint-
brush and was putting in every kind of
chiaroscuro while she, helplessly, looked on.
Now it was the grey of disillusion, now the
high light of faith. The picture shaped it-

26

self under her eyes. She tried to direct him, but he had bolted with her. "Ten days ago," she tried to say, "you didn't know me." And, to make matters more disconcerting, Lomax himself was evidently in some great distress. He seemed to be impelled by some inner fire to pronounce the words he was pronouncing; to be abandoning all egoism under the exaltation of self-sacrifice. The absurd creature believed in his mission. And Miss Whitaker was not slow to kindle at his flame. They were both caught up, now, in their own drama. Intent, he urged details from her, and with now a sigh escaping her, and now a little flare of pride, she hinted confirmation. It was really admirable, the background which between them they contrived to build up; personalities emerged, three-dimensional; Ecuador fell into its place with a click. Even the expedition to Egypt fitted in—Miss Whitaker had accepted Bellamy's invitation in order to escape the vigilance of a brother. He had a hot temper, this brother—Robert; any affront to his sister, and he would be flying off to Ecuador. Robert was immensely wealthy; he owned an oil-field in Persia; he would spare no expense in searching Ecuador from end to end. He had already been known to scour Russia to avenge a woman. By this time Lomax was himself ready to scour Ecuador. Miss Whitaker wavered; she relished the idea of a Lomax with smoking nostrils ransacking Central America, but on second thoughts she dissuaded him; she didn't want, she said, to send him to his death. Lomax had an idea that the man— still anonymous—would not prove so formidable. Miss Whitaker constructed him as very formidable indeed; one of the world's bad lots, but in every sense of the word irresistible. Lomax scorned the adjective; he had no use, he said, for bad lots so callous as to lay the sole burden of con-

Lomax was, for they had long since settled that it was better for them not to communicate. He would see the death in the papers, of course, and perhaps he would write her a formal letter of condolence, but she knew she could trust him not to come near her until she sent for him. This was April; in October she would send. Then she was startled by a faint throaty sound, and saw that the fingers which had been picking the blankets were once convulsed, and then lay still.

The *Nereid* set sail from Alexandria two days later. Bellamy did not seem able to make up his mind where he wanted to go. Sicily was talked of, the Dalmatian coast, the Piraeus, and Constantinople. The others were quite passive under his vacillations. Now they were afloat, and had re-entered that self-contained little world which is in every ship at sea; temporary, but with so convincing an illusion of permanence; a world weighing so many tons, confined within a measure of so many paces, limited to a population of so many souls, a world at the same time restricted and limitless, here closely bound by the tiny compass of the ship, and there subject to no frontiers but those of the watery globe itself. In a ship at sea our land life slips away, and our existence fills with the new conditions. Moreover in a sailing ship the governing laws are few and simple; a mere question of elements. Bellamy was sailor enough—eccentric enough, said some—to despise auxiliary steam. Appreciative of caprice, in the wind he found a spirit capricious enough to satisfy his taste. In a calm he was patient, and in a storm amused, and for the rest he comported himself in this matter, as in all others (according to his set and general principle), as though he had the whole leisure of life before him.

No shore was visible, for Bellamy liked to

keep the shore out of sight. It increased, he explained, not only the sense of space but also the sense of time. So they lounged along, having the coasts of Barbary somewhere over the horizon, and being pleasantly independent of century; indeed, the hours of their meals were of greater import to them than the interval elapsed since the birth of Christ. This, Bellamy said, was the wholesome attitude. Bellamy, in his courteous, sophisticated, and ironical way, was ever so slightly a tyrant. He did not dictate to them, but he suggested, not only where they should go, but also what they should think. It was very subtly done. There was not enough, not nearly enough, for them to resent; there was only enough to make them, sometimes, for a skimming moment, uneasy. What if Bellamy, when they wanted to go home, wouldn't go home? What if, from being a host, he should slide into being a jailer?

35

But in the meantime it was pleasant enough to cruise in the *Nereid*, lying in deck-chairs, while Bellamy, with his hand on the helm and the great blade of the mainsail above him, watched from under the peak of his cap, not them, but the sea.

Very blue it was too, and the *Nereid*, when she was not running before a fair wind on an even keel, lay over to the water, so low that now and then she shipped a gobbet of sea, only a thin little runnel that escaped at once through the open scuppers of the lee runner, in a hurry to get back to its element. Bellamy was bored by a fair wind; he hated the monotony of a day with the sheet out and the beautiful scooped shape of the spinnaker, and the crew asleep for'ard, since there was no handling of gear to keep them on the run. What he liked was a day with plenty of tacking, and then he would turn the mate or the captain off and take the wheel himself, and cry "Lee-o!" to the crew.

36

And what pleased him even better was to catch the eye of the mate and give the order with only a nod of the head, so that his unwarned guests slithered across the deck as the ship went about, when he would laugh and apologise with perfect urbanity; but they noticed that next time he had the chance he did precisely the same thing again. "Bellamy likes teasing us," said Lomax, with a good deal of meaning in his tone. Bellamy did, even by so slight an irritation. And once he brought off a Dutchman's gybe, which nearly shot Lomax, who was lying asleep under the mizzen-boom, into the sea.

One sleeps a great part of the time on a yacht. Artivale fished, and dissected the fish he caught, so that a section of the deck was strewn with little ribs and spines. Lomax surveyed these through his spectacles. Artivale had long slim fingers, and he took up and set down the little bones, fitting them together, with the dexterity of a lace-maker

37

among her bobbins. Tailor-wise he sat, his hair lifted by the wind, and sometimes he looked up with a full smile into the disapproving face of Miss Whitaker. "Play spillikins, Miss Whitaker?" he asked, jumbling his fish bones all together into a heap.

Very blue and white it all was. Soft, immense white clouds floated, and the sails were white, and Artivale's tiny graveyard, but the scrubbed deck, which in Southampton Water had looked white, here appeared pale yellow by contrast. The sails threw blue shadows. The crew ran noiselessly on bare feet. "When shall we get there?" Lomax wondered, but since he did not know where "there" was, and since all the blueness and whiteness were to him overlaid as with the angry cloud of an impending storm, he was content to hammock himself passively in the amplitude of enveloping time. He was, indeed, in no hurry, for his land-life, now withdrawn, had been merely a thing to be

38

got through; he had an idle curiosity to see what was going to happen in these changed aeons that stretched before him; nor did he know that Marion Vane's husband was dead. So he lay in his deck-chair, speculating about Bellamy, watching Artivale, aware of the parallel proximity of Miss Whitaker—who was his wife—in *her* deck-chair, and occasionally, by way of refreshment, turning his eyes behind their owlish spectacles over the expanse of his lurid sea and sky.

What of it, anyway? There were quite a number of other communities in the world besides this little community, microscopic on the Mediterranean. Lomax saw the blue as it was not, the others saw or thought they saw the blue as it was, but unless and until our means of communication become more subtle than they at present are, we cannot even be sure that our eyes see colours alike. How, then, should we know one another? Lomax lived alone with his secret, Bellamy

with his; and as for Miss Whitaker, if Truth
be indeed accustomed to dwell at the bottom
of a well, at the bottom of Miss Whitaker's
heart she must surely have found a dwelling
suited to her taste. Artivale, being a scientist intent upon a clue, probably knew more
of the secrets of life than the seamen who
begot their offspring in the rude old fashion,
but it is to be doubted whether even Artivale
knew much that was worth knowing. He
claimed to have produced a tadpole by ecto-
genetic birth, but, having produced it, he was
quite unable to tell that tadpole whither it
was going when it inconsiderately died, and,
moreover, as he himself observed, there were
tadpoles enough in the world already.

Volcanic islands began, pitting the sea;
white towns and golden temples clung to a
violet coast. Bellamy suggested to them
that they did not want to land, a suggestion
in which they acquiesced. They shared a
strange disinclination to cross Bellamy.

They were sailing now within a stone's
throw of a wild, precipitous coast, their
nights and their days boundaried by magnificent sunsets and splendid dawns. But
for those, time did not exist. Geography did
not exist either; Bellamy referred to Illyria,
and they were content to leave it at that. It
fitted in with the unreality of their voyage.
There are paintings of ships setting sail into
a haze of sunlight, ships full-rigged, broad-
beamed, with tracery of rope, pushing off for
the unknown, voyages to Cythera, misty and
romantic; Lomax wore the amber spectacles,
and saw a golden ship evanescent in golden
air. Morning and evening flamed upon the
sea; each day was a lagoon of blue. Islets
and rocks stained the shield of water; mountains swept down and trod the sea; cities
of Illyria rose upon the breast of the coast-
line; rose; drew near; and faded past.
Venice and Byzantium in spire and cupola
clashed the arms of peace for ever on the

41

scene of their exploits. But towns were rare; they passed not more than one in every four-and-twenty hours. For the rest, they were alone with that piratical seaboard descending barbarously to the sea; never a hut, never a road, never a goat to hint at life, but caves and creeks running between the headlands, and sullen mountains like a barrier between the water and the inland tracts. The little ship sailed lonely beneath the peaks. Day after day she sailed, idly coasting Illyria, and Bellamy waited for the storm. "Treacherous waters," he had observed on entering them. Indeed it seemed incongruous that the sea should be so calm and the shore so wild. Day after day unbroken, with that angry coast always on their right hand and the placid sea on their left; day after day of leisure, with a wall of disaster banking higher and higher against them.

Those paintings of ships show the ship

42

setting sail in fair weather; they never fol-
low her into the turbulence of her adventure.
Friends speed her with waving handker-
chiefs, and turn away, and know nothing of
her till a letter comes saying that she has
arrived at her place of port. And, for the
matter of that, the lives of friends touch here
and there in the same fashion, and the
gap over the interval is never bridged,
knowledge being but a splintered mirror
which shall never gather to a smooth and
even surface.

The *Nereid*, then, with her living freight,
saw the serenity of Illyria broken up into a
night of anger, but the wives of the crew,
lighting their lamps in brick cottages at
Brightlingsea, knew nothing of it, and the
wife of the captain writing to her aunt said,
"Joe has a nice job with a gentleman name
of Bellamy on a yorl in the Meddingterra-
nean," and Marion Vane with an edging of
white lawn to her mourning at neck and cuffs

43

was vague to her trustee at dinner regarding the disposal of her country house, for she believed that this time next year she would be married to Lomax. The *Nereid* was not broad-beamed; she was slim as a hound, and it was not with a plebeian solidity but with an aristocratic mettle that she took the storm. Her canvas rapidly furled, she rode with bare masts crazily sawing the sky. Black ragged night enveloped her; the coast, although invisible, contributed to the tempest, throwing its boulders against the waves as the waves hurled themselves against its boulders. The little boat, a thing of naught, was battered at that meeting-place of enemies. Rain and spray drove together across the deck, as momently the storm increased and the wind tore howling through the naked spars. The men were black figures clinging to stays for support, going down with the ship when she swooped from the crest down into the trough, rising again with her, thank-

44

ful to find the deck still there beneath their feet, lashed by the rain, blinded by the darkness, unable to see, able only to feel, whether with their hands that, wet and frozen, clung to rail and stanchion, or with their bodies that sank and rose, enduring the tremendous buffeting of the tossing ship, and the shock of water that, as it broke over the deck, knocked the breath from their lungs and all but swept them from their refuge into the hopeless broiling of the sea.

Lomax was in the deck-house. There, he was dry, and could prop himself to resist the rearing and plunging; and could almost enjoy, moreover, the drench of water flung against the little hutch, invisible, but mighty and audible, streaming away after sweeping the ship from end to end. A funny lot they would be to drown, he reflected; and he remembered their departure from Southampton, all a little shy and constrained, with Miss Whitaker sprightly but on the defensive. How long ago that was, he failed to calculate. They had drifted down to Calshot, anchoring there on a washed April evening, between a liquid sky and oily lagoon-like reaches, gulls and sea-planes skimming sea and heaven, in the immense primrose peace of sunset. And they had known nothing of one another, and Miss Whitaker had written letters after dinner in the saloon. Well, well! thought Lomax.

There came a fumbling at the deck-house door, a sudden blast of wind, a shower of spray, and Bellamy, in glistening oilskins, scrambled into the shelter, slamming the door behind him. A pool began to gather immediately round him on the floor. Lomax thought that he looked strangely triumphant,—as though this were his hour. "Glad to have got us all into this mess," he thought meanly. It aggravated him that he should never yet have found the key to Bellamy.

46

"I want to talk to you," cried Bellamy, rocking on his feet as he stood.

He wanted to talk. External danger, then, gave him internal courage.

"Come into my cabin," he cried to Lomax over his shoulder, as he began to make his way down the companion.

But Lomax, really, knew nothing of all this. The storm, really, had not entered his consciousness at all; Bellamy, and Bellamy alone, had occupied it all the while. All that he knew, really, was that he found himself in Bellamy's cabin.

In Bellamy's cabin, everything loose had been stowed away, so that it was bare of personal possessions; the narrow bunk, the swinging lamp, the closed cupboards alone remained untouched in the cabin that had sheltered the privacy of Bellamy's midnight hours. Lomax, as he lurched in through the door and was violently thrown against the

47

bunk, reflected that he had never before set foot in the owner's quarters. They were small, low, and seamanlike; no luxury of chintz softened the plain wooden fittings; Lomax forgot the delicate yacht, and saw himself only in the presence of a sailor aboard his vessel, for Bellamy in his sou'-wester and streaming oilskins, straddling in sea-boots beneath the lamp, had more the aspect of a captain newly descended from the bridge than of the millionaire owner of a pleasure yawl. He kept his feet, too, in spite of the violent motion, while Lomax, clinging to the side of the bunk, could barely save himself from being flung again across the cabin. But Bellamy stood there full of triumph, fully alive for the first time since Lomax had known him; his courteous languor dropped from him, he looked like a happy man. "This weather suits you," Lomax shouted above the din.

The yacht strained and creaked; now she

lifted high on a wave, now fell sickeningly down into the trough. Water dashed against the closed port-hole and streamed past as the ship rose again to take the wave. Cast about in all directions, now dipping with her bows, now rolling heavily from furrow to furrow, she floundered with no direction and with no purpose other than to keep afloat; govern herself she could not, but maintain her hold on life she would. Lomax, who in the cabin down below could see nothing of the action of the sea, felt only the ship shaken in an angry hand, and heard the crash of tumult as the seas struck down upon the deck. "Will she live through it?" he screamed.

"If she isn't driven ashore," cried Bellamy with perfect indifference. "Come nearer; we can't make ourselves heard in this infernal noise."

It did not occur to him to move nearer to Lomax; perhaps he took pride in standing in the middle of the cabin, under the lamp now madly swaying in its gimbals, with the water still dripping from his oilskins into a pool on the floor. Lomax staggered towards him, clinging on to the edge of the bunk. It crossed his mind that this was a strange occasion to choose for conversation, but his standard of strangeness being by now somewhat high he did not pause for long to consider that.

"I want to have a talk with you," said Bellamy again.

An enormous shock of water struck the ship overhead, and for a moment she quivered through all her timbers,—a moment of stillness almost, while she ceased to roll, and nothing but that shudder ran through her. "Stood that well," said Bellamy, listening. Then she plunged; plunged as though never to rise any more, falling down as though a trap in the waters had opened to receive her; but she came up, lifted as rapidly as she had

wet, and the lamp over his head gleamed upon his thick white hair and carved the shadows of weariness on his face, shadows that moved and shifted with the swinging of the lamp. "I was inconsiderate, doubtless,—exasperating,—wouldn't make plans, —I owe you all an apology. I am an egoist, you see, Lomax. I was thinking of myself. There were certain things I wanted to allow myself the luxury of forgetting."

It was intolerable that Bellamy should heap this blame upon himself.

"You teased us," muttered Lomax in shamed justification.

"Yes, I teased you," said Bellamy. "I apologise again. I disturbed your comfort. But knowing myself to be a dying man, I indulged myself in that mischief. I had moods, I confess, when the sight of your comfort and your security irritated me even into the desire to drown you all. It's bad thinking, of a very elementary sort, and the

53

foundation of most cynicism. I accept your rebuke."

"Damn you," said Lomax, twisting his hands.

"Nevertheless," Bellamy continued, "I shan't scruple to ask of you the favour I was going to ask. I am a coward, Lomax. I am afraid of pain. I am afraid of disease,— of long, slow, disgusting disease—you understand me? And I have long been looking for some one who, when the moment came, would put me out of it."

"You can count on me," said Lomax. At the same time he could not help hoping that the moment had not come there and then. Procrastination and a carefully chosen pair of spectacles would make him a very giant of decision.

Lomax went up on deck; he wanted a storm outside his head as well as a storm within it. The rain had ceased, and the tall spars swayed across a cloudy sky,

rent between the clouds to show the moon.
The sea was very rough and beautiful beneath the moon. It was good to see the
storm at last, to see as well as to feel. Stars
appeared, among the rack of the clouds, and
vaguely astronomical phrases came into
Lomax's mind: Nebulæ, Inter-planetary
space, Asteroids, Eighty thousand miles a
second; he supposed that there were men to
whom trillions were a workable reality, just
as there were men who could diagnose Bellamy's disease and give him his sentence of
death for the sum of two guineas. Two
guineas was a contemptible sum to Bellamy,
who was so rich a man. To Artivale, what
did two guineas mean? A new retort? A
supply of chemical? And to Lomax himself,—a new pair of glasses? Tossed on
Illyrian billows, he saw a lunar rainbow
standing suddenly upon the waves, amaz-
ingly coloured in the night of black and
silver. Life jumbled madly in his brain.

There was Marion, too, lost to him from the moment he had stepped out of that system in which existence was simply a thing to be got through as inconspicuously as possible; and leaning against the deck-house for support he came nearer to tears than he had ever been in his life.

Of course it was to be expected that the death of so wealthy a man as Bellamy should create a certain sensation. There were head-lines in the papers, and Arthur Lomax, who had dined with him that evening and had been the last person to see him alive, spent tiresome days evading reporters. Veronal it was; no question or doubt about that; the tumbler containing the dregs of poison and the dregs of whisky and soda was found quite frankly standing on the table beside him. Lomax's evidence at the inquest threw no light on the suicide; no, Mr. Bellamy had not appeared depressed; yes, Mr. Bellamy

56

had mixed a whisky and soda and drunk it off in his, Lomax's, presence. He had not seen Mr. Bellamy add anything to the contents of the tumbler. He was unable to say whether Mr. Bellamy had mixed a second whisky and soda after he, Lomax, had left the house. What time had he left? Late; about one in the morning. They had sat up talking. No, he had not known Mr. Bellamy very long, but they had been for a yachting cruise together, lasting some weeks. He would not say that they had become intimate. He knew nothing of Mr. Bellamy's private affairs. He had been very much shocked to read of the death next morning in the papers. Thank you, Mr. Lomax, that will do.

Bellamy was buried, and Lomax, Artivale, and Miss Whitaker attended the funeral, drawn together again into their little group of four,—if you counted Bellamy, invisible, but terribly present, in his coffin. To be

57

buried in the rain is dreary, but to be buried
on a morning of gay sunshine is more ironical. Fortunately for Lomax, he was able
to obscure the sunshine by the use of his
black glasses; and heaven knows he needed
them. He was either indifferent or oblivious
to the remarkable appearance he offered, in
a top-hat, a black coat, and black spectacles.
"Weak eyes," noted the reporters. In fact
he cared nothing for externals now, especially with the memory of his last meeting
with Bellamy strong upon him. On seeing
Miss Whitaker he roused himself a little,
just enough to look at her with a wondering
curiosity; he had forgotten her existence lately, except for the dim but constant knowledge that something stood blocked between
him and Marion Vane, a something that
wore neither name nor features, and whose
materialisation he recognised, briefly puz-
zled by her importance, as Miss Whitaker.
Important yet not important, for, in the

58

ruin? Why should reality recede? What
was reality? Marion with her hands outstretched; so sure of him. Better to have
helped Bellamy; better to have helped Miss
Whitaker. Even though Miss Whitaker's
need of help was, perhaps, fictitious? Yes,
even so. The loss was hers, not his. Her
falsity could not impair his quixotism; that
was a wild, irrational thing, separate, untouched, independent. It flamed out of
his life,—for all the unreality of Miss
Whitaker, that actual Miss Whitaker who
subscribed to the census paper, paid rates
and taxes, and had an existence in the eyes
of the law,—it flamed as a few things
flamed: his two meetings with Bellamy, his
repudiation of Marion Vane. There were
just a few gashes of life, bitten in; that was
all one could hope for. Was it worth living
seventy, eighty years, to accumulate half-a-
dozen scars? Half-a-dozen ineradicable
pictures, scattered over the monotony of

seventy, eighty pages. He had known, when he married Miss Whitaker, that he repudiated Marion Vane; to repudiate her when she came with outstretched hands was but the projection of the half-hour in the Cairo registry office. But it was that that he remembered, and her hurt incredulous eyes; as it was Bellamy's cry that he remembered; always the tangible thing,—such was the weakness of the human, fleshly system. Now, Bellamy would rot and be eaten, "Earth to earth, dust to dust"; his sickly body corrupting within the senseless coffin; and by that Lomax would be haunted, rather than by his spiritual tragedy; the tangible again, in the worms crawling in and out of a brain its master had preferred to still into eternal nescience. How long did it take for the buried flesh to become a skeleton? So long, and no less, would Lomax be haunted by the rotting corpse of Bellamy, as he would not have been haunted by the man dragging poked the fire. But her past stretched away behind her, a blank to Lomax. No doubt she had done sums, worn a pig-tail, cried, and had a mother. So far, conjectures were safe. But her emotional interludes? All locked up? or hadn't there been any? What, to her, was the half-hour in the Cairo registry office? Did it bulk, to her, as Bellamy and Marion Vane bulked to him? One could never feel the shape of another person's mind; never justly apprehend its population. And he was not at all anxious to plumb the possibly abysmal pathos of Miss Whitaker; he didn't want those friends of hers, those strong manly men, to evaporate beneath the crudity of his search. He didn't want to be faced with the true desolation of the little room.

The rumours about Bellamy's death became common property only a few weeks later. They apparently had their origin in

Bellamy's will, by which the fortune went to Lomax, turning him from a poor man into a rich one, to his embarrassed astonishment. He wondered vaguely whether the rumours had been set afoot by Miss Whitaker, but came to the conclusion that fact or what she believed to be fact had less allurement for her than frank fiction. Ergo, he said, her seducer in Ecuador interests her more than her secret husband in London. And he reasoned well.

Bellamy's body was exhumed. No one understood why, since the administration of veronal had never been disputed. It was exhumed secretly, at night, by the light of a lantern, and carried into an empty cottage next to the graveyard. The papers next day gave these details. Lomax read them with a nauseous horror. Bellamy, who had abjured life so that his tormented body might be at peace! And now, surrounded by constables, officers of the Law, on a rainy night, lit by the gleams of a hurricane lantern, what remained of his flesh had been smuggled into a derelict cottage and investigated by the scalpel of the anatomist. Truly the grave was neither fine nor private.

Then the newspaper accounts ceased; Bellamy was reburied; and the world went on as usual.

A friendship flared up—surely the queerest in London,—between Lomax and Miss Whitaker. They met quite often. They dined together; they went to theatres. One afternoon they chartered a taxi and did a London round: they went to Sir John Soane's Museum, to Mme. Tussaud's, and the Zoo. Side by side, they looked at Mme. Tussaud's own modelling of Marie Antoinette's severed head fresh from the basket; they listened to somebody's cook beside them, reading from her catalogue: "Mary Antonette, gelatined in 1792; Lewis sixteen,

—why, he was gelatined too"; they held their noses in the Small Cats' House, appreciated the Coati, who can turn his long snout up or down, to left or right, without moving his head, and contemplated at length the Magnificent Bird of Paradise, who hopped incessantly, and the Frogmouth, who, of all creation, has in the supremest degree the quality of immobility and identification with his bough. Lomax found Miss Whitaker quite companionable on these occasions. If she told him how often she had observed the Magnificent Bird and the Frogmouth in their native haunts, he liked her none the less for that; a piquancy was added to her otherwise drab little personality, for he was convinced that she had never stirred out of England save in Bellamy's yacht. And certainly there had been neither Magnificent Bird nor Frogmouth in Illyria.

How romantic were the journeys of

Miss Whitaker! How picturesque her travelling companions!

It must not be thought, however, that she incessantly talked about herself, for the very reverse was true; the allusions which she let fall were few, but although few they were always most startling.

Her company was usually, if not immediately, available. That was a great advantage to Lomax, who soon found that he could depend upon her almost at a moment's notice. Sometimes, indeed, a little obstacle came back to him over the telephone: "Lunch to-day? oh dear, I am so sorry I can't; I promised Roger that I would lunch with him," or else, "I promised Carmen that I would motor down to Kew." Lomax would express his regret. And Miss Whitaker, "But wait a moment, if you will ring off now I will try to get through to him (or her), and see if I can put it off." And twenty minutes later Lomax's telephone bell

would ring, and Miss Whitaker would tell
him how angry Roger (or Carmen) had
been, declaring that she was really too insuf-
ferable, and that he (or she) would have
nothing more to do with her.

Miss Whitaker, indeed, was part of the
fantasy of Lomax's life. He took a great
interest in Roger and Carmen, and was never
tired of their doings or their tempers. He
sometimes arrived at Miss Whitaker's house
to find a used tea-cup on the tray, which was
pointed out to him as evidence of their recent
departure. He sympathised over a bruise
inflicted by the jealousy of Roger. On the
whole, he preferred Carmen, for he liked
women to have pretty hands, and Carmen's
were small, southern, and dimpled; in fact,
he came very near to being in love with Carmen. He beheld them, of course, as he now
beheld Miss Whitaker, as he beheld everything, through the miraculous veil of his
spectacles; crudity was tempered, criticism

in abeyance; only compassion remained, and a vast indifference. All sense of reality had finally left him on the day that he repudiated Marion Vane; he scarcely suffered now, and even the nightmare which was beginning to hem him in held no personal significance; he was withdrawn. He heard the rumours about Bellamy's death, as though they concerned another man. He was quite sure that he regretted nothing he had done.

He was staring at the card he held in his hand: MR. ROBERT WHITAKER.

So Robert existed. Robert who had scoured Russia to avenge a woman. He was disappointed in Miss Whitaker. Since Robert existed, what need had she to mention him? An imaginary brother might tickle the fancy; a real brother was merely commonplace. With a sigh he gave orders for the admission of Robert. He awaited him, reflecting that the mortification of discovering that which one believed true to be

71

untrue is as nothing compared to the mortification of discovering that which one believed untrue to be true. All art, said
Lomax, is a lie; but that lie contains more
truth than the truth. But here was Robert.

He was large and angry; lamentably like
his sister's presentment of him. Lomax
began to believe both in his Persian oil-field
and in his exaggerated sense of honour. And
when he heard Robert's business, he could
no longer cherish any doubts as to Miss
Whitaker's veracity. Here was Robert,
large as life, and unmistakably out for
revenge.

Lomax sat smiling, examining his finger-
nails, and assenting to everything. Yes,
he had been secretly married to Robert's
sister in Cairo. Yes, it was quite possible, if Robert liked to believe it, that he
was a bigamist. A seducer of young women.
At that Lomax frankly laughed. Robert did
not at all like the note in his laughter;

72

mocking? satirical? He did not like it at all. Did Mr. Lomax at least realise that he would have Miss Whitaker's family to reckon with? He, Robert, had heard things lately about Mr. Lomax which he would not specify at present, but which would be investigated, with possibly very unpleasant results for Mr. Lomax. They were things which were making Miss Whitaker's family most uneasy. He did not pretend to know what Mr. Lomax's little game had been, but he had come to-day to warn him that he had better lie low and be up to no tricks. Lomax was greatly amused to find himself regarded as an adventurer. He put on a bland manner towards Robert which naturally strengthened Robert's conviction. And his last remark persuaded Robert that he was not only dangerous, but eccentric.

"By the way," he said, stopping Robert at the door, "would you mind telling me whether you have ever been in Russia? And did you catch your man?"

Robert stared angrily, and said, "Yes, to both questions."

"Ah, pity, pity!" said Lomax regretfully, shaking his head. There was another illusion gone.

He was almost tempted to wonder whether he ought not to believe again, as he had believed originally, in the seducer in Ecuador.

When he next saw Miss Whitaker he made no allusion to Robert's visit; neither did she, though she must have known of it. She had received an anonymous letter threatening abduction, and was full of that; she showed it to Lomax, who considered it with suitable gravity. He found Miss Whitaker's adventures most precious to him in his state of life and of mind. He clung on to them, for he knew that his own danger was becoming urgent. He had heard the phrase, "living on a volcano," but until now it had had as little meaning as it has for the rest of us. But now he knew well enough the expectation of being blown, at any moment, sky-high.

With these thoughts in his head, Lomax decided that he must see Artivale before it was too late. Before it was too late. Before, that is to say, he had been deprived of the liberty of action; that was the first step, that deprivation, to be followed by the second step: deprived of speech, gesture, thought,—deprived of life itself. Before he was reduced, first to a prisoner, and then to a limp body lifted from under the gallows by the hands of men.

He must see Artivale.

Artivale lived in Paris. Lomax travelled to Paris, surprised, almost, to find his passport unchallenged and himself unchecked as he climbed into a train or crossed the gangway of a boat. Again and again surprise returned to him, whether he ordered a cup of tea in his Pullman or sat in his corner of the French compartment looking at *La Vie Parisienne* like any ordinary man. He was going to Paris. He had bought his ticket, and the clerk in the booking-office had handed it to him without comment. That meant freedom—being a free man. The privileges of freedom. He looked at his fellow-travellers and wondered whether they knew how free they were. How free to come and go, and how quickly their freedom might be snatched from them. He wondered what they would say if they knew that a condemned man travelled with them. Time was the important thing; whether he had time enough to do what he had to do before the hand fell upon him. "But," thought Lomax, laughing to himself, "they are all condemned, only they forget about it; they know it, but they forget." And as he looked

76

at them through his spectacles,—the black ones,—moving as though they had eternity before them in a world dim, unreal, and subdued, they seemed to him in their preoccupation and their forgetfulness extremely pitiful.

Under the great girders of the Gare du Nord they scurried, tiny figures galvanised suddenly into shouting and haste. But it was not the recollection of their ultimate condemnation that made them hurry; it was the returning urgency of their own affairs after the passivity of the journey. After all, the train is going as fast as it can, and the most impatient traveller can do no more than allow himself to be carried. But on arrival it is different. Porters may be speeded up by abuse, other travellers may be shoved out of the way, one may capture the first taxi in the rank rather than the last. All these things are of great importance. Perversely, Lomax, as soon as he had de-

scended from the train, began to dawdle.
The station, that great cavern full of
shadows, swallowing up the gleaming tracks,
stopping the monstrous trains as with a wall
of finality; those tiny figures so senselessly
hurrying; those loads of humanity dis-
charged out of trains from unknown origins
towards unknown destinations; all this appeared to him as the work of some crazy
etcher, building up a system of lit or darkened masses, here a column curving into
relief, there a cavernous exit yawning to
engulf, here groins and iron arches soaring
to a very heaven of night, there metallic per-
spectives diminishing towards a promise of
day; and everywhere the tiny figures streaming beneath the architectural nightmare,
microscopic bodies of men with faces undis-
tinguishable, flying as for their lives along
passage-ways between eddies of smoke in a
fantastic temple of din and murk and ma-
chinery. Moreover, he was wearing, it must

78

be remembered, the black glasses. That which was sombre enough to other eyes, to him was sinister as the pit. He knew the mood which the black glasses induced; yet he had deliberately come away with no other pair in his pocket. The fear which troubled him most was the thought that in his imprisonment his glasses might be taken from him,—he had dim recollections, survivals from a life in which the possibility of imprisonment played no part, that condemned criminals must be deprived of all instruments of suicide. And the black glasses, of them all, best suited his natural humour. Therefore he had indulged himself, on perhaps his last opportunity, by bringing no alternative pair. Since he had lost everything in life, he would riot in the luxury of beholding life through an extravagance of darkness.

A dragon pursued him, clanging a bell; mechanically he moved aside, and the electric luggage-trucks passed him, writhing into the customs-house at the end of the station. Artivale lived in the Quartier Latin; it was necessary to get there before the hand fell on his shoulder. Paris taxi-drivers were mad, surely, and their taxis on the verge of disintegration; chasing enormous trams, charged by demoniac lorries, hooting incessantly and incessantly hooted at, Lomax in his wheeled scrap-iron rattled across a Paris darkened into the menace of an imminent cataclysm. A heaven of lead hung over the ghastly streets. All condemned, thought Lomax, as he racketed through the procession of life that was so gaily unconscious of the night in which it moved.

He arrived at Artivale's house.

Artivale himself opened the door.

"Good God!" he said on seeing Lomax, "what . . . But come in.—You're ill," he continued, when he had got Lomax inside the door.

"No," said Lomax, oblivious of the startling appearance he presented, with haggard cheeks behind the absurd spectacles; "only, I had to see you,—in a hurry."

"In a hurry?" said Artivale, accustomed to think of Lomax as a man without engagements, occupations, or urgency.

"You see," said Lomax, "I murdered Bellamy and I may be arrested at any moment."

"Of course that does explain your hurry," said Artivale, "but would you mind coming down to the kitchen, where I want to keep my eye on some larvae? We can talk there. My servants don't understand English."

Lomax followed him downstairs to the basement, where in a vaulted kitchen enormous blue butterflies circled in the air and a stout negress stoked the oven. The room was dark and excessively hot. "We're in the tropics," said Lomax, looking at the butterflies.

Artivale apologised for the atmosphere.

81

"I have to keep it hot for the sake of the larvae," he explained, "and I had to import the black women because no French servant would stand the heat. These are the larvae," and he showed Lomax various colourless smudges lying on the tables and the dresser. "Now tell me about Bellamy."

The negress beamed upon them benevolently, showing her teeth. A negro girl came from an inner room, carrying a pile of plates. A butterfly of extraordinary brilliancy quivered for a moment on the kitchen clock, and swept away, up into the shadows of the roof, fanning Lomax with its wings in passing.

"The murder was nothing," said Lomax; "he asked me to do it. He was ill, you see,—mortally,—and he was afraid of pain. That's all very simple. He left me his fortune, though."

"Yes," said Artivale, "I read his will in the paper."

82

"I am leaving that to you," said Lomax.

"To me,—but, my dear fellow, you're not going to die."

"Oh yes," said Lomax, "I shall be hung, of course. Besides, we are all condemned, you know."

"Ultimately, yes," replied Artivale, "but not imminently."

"That's why people forget about it," said Lomax, gazing at him very intently.

Artivale began to wonder whether Lomax suffered from delusions.

"Could you take off those spectacles?" he asked.

"No," said Lomax. "I should go mad if I did. You have no idea how beautiful your butterflies are, seen through them,—the blue through a veil of black. But to go back to the fortune. I ought, perhaps, to leave it to Miss Whitaker, but she has enough of her own already."

83

"Why to Miss Whitaker?" asked Artivale.

"I married her in Cairo," replied Lomax; "I forgot to tell you that. It is so difficult to remember all these things."

"Are you telling me that you and Miss Whitaker were married all that time on the yacht?"

"Exactly. She was going to have a child, you know,—by another man."

"I see," said Artivale.

"But of course all these things that I am telling you are private."

"Oh, quite," said Artivale. "Miss Whitaker was going to have a child, so you married her; Bellamy had a mortal illness, so you murdered him. Private and confidential. I quite understand."

"I hope you will have no scruples about accepting the fortune," said Lomax anxiously. "I am leaving it to you, really, as I should leave it to a scientific institute,—

because I believe you will use it to the good of humanity. But if you make any difficulties I shall alter my will and leave it to the Royal Society."

"Tell me, Lomax," said Artivale, "do you care a fig for humanity?"

"There is nothing else to care about," said Lomax.

"Of course I accept your offer,—though not for myself," said Artivale.

"That's all right then," said Lomax, and he rose to go.

"Stay a moment," said Artivale. "Naturally, you got Bellamy to sign a paper stating that you were about to murder him at his own request?"

"No," said Lomax; "it did cross my mind, but it seemed indelicate, somehow,—egotistic, you know, at a moment like that, to mention such a thing,—and as he didn't suggest it I thought I wouldn't bother him.

85

After all, he was paying me a great compliment,—a very great compliment."

"Oh, undoubtedly!" said Artivale, "but I think, if you will forgive my saying so, that your delicacy outran your prudence. Any evidence that I can give . . ."

"But you have only my word, and that isn't evidence," replied Lomax, smiling.

At that moment a bell pealed through the house upstairs.

"That will be for me," said Lomax; "how lucky that I had time to say what I wanted to say."

"Oh, you *are* lucky, aren't you?" cried Artivale wildly; "a lucky, lucky dog. Your luck's inconceivable. Lomax,—look here,— Lomax,—you must get out of this house. The back door . . ."

The bell rang again.

"It's only a question of sooner or later," said Lomax gently; "for everybody, you know; not only for me. If they let me keep

86

the spectacles I don't mind. With them, I
don't see things as they are. Or perhaps I
do. It doesn't make much difference which.
If you won't go up and open that door, I
shall go and open it myself."

They took Lomax away in a cab. He was
not allowed to keep his spectacles. Artivale
came downstairs again to the kitchen, and
watched a peacock butterfly of humming-
bird proportions crawl free of its cocoon and
spread its wings in flight.

It was only during the course of his trial
that Lomax discovered how pitiable a
weapon was truth. A law-court is a place
of many contradictions; pitch-pine walls and
rows of benches give it the appearance of a
school treat, white wigs and scarlet and
phraseology erect it into a seeming monu-
ment to all civilisation, but of the helpless-
ness of the victim there is at least no doubt
at all. His bewilderment is the one certain

factor. Lomax in the days when he might meet fact with fantasy had been a contented man; now, when he tried to meet with fact the fantastical world which so suddenly and so utterly swamped him, was a man confounded, a man floundering for a foothold. He had lost his spectacles. He had lost his attitude towards life. He had lost Miss Whitaker, or at any rate had exchanged her for a Miss Whitaker new and formidable, a Miss Whitaker who, astonishingly and catastrophically, spoke a portion of the truth. If earth had turned to heaven and heaven to earth a greater chaos could not have resulted in his mind.

The public see me in the dock; they do not see me in my cell. Let me look at the walls; they are white, not clouded into a nameless colour, as once they would have been. Uncompromisingly white. How ugly, how bare! But I must remember: this is a prison cell. I have no means of turning it into anything else. I am a prisoner on trial for my life. That's fact. A plain man, suffering the consequences for the actions of a creature enchanted, now disappeared. The white walls are fact. Geometry is a fact,— or so they say,—but didn't some one suggest that in another planetary system the laws of geometry might be reversed? This cell is geometrical; square floor, square ceiling, square walls, square window intersected by bars. Geometrical shadows, Euclidean angles. White light. Did I, or did I not, do this, that, and the other? I did, but . . . No buts. Facts are facts. Yes or no. Geometrical questions require geometrical answers. If A be equal to B, then C . . . But either I am mad, or they are mad, or the King's English no longer means what it used to mean.

In the dock again. Amazing statements, in substance true, in essence madly false. He must neither interrupt nor attempt to justify. All these events, which dance round him pointing crooked fingers, disfiguring their aspects into such caricatures, all these events came about so naturally, so inevitably. He knows that, as a lesson learnt, though the enchantment is gone from him. If he might speak, even, what should he relate of that experience? If he might speak! But when he speaks he damns himself. His counsel speaks for him, well-primed, so far as his client's idea of honour has been allowed to prime him; but Lomax knows all the time that his life is of no real consequence to his counsel, except in so far as success provides advertisement; he knows that after the trial is over, one way or the other, his counsel will meet the opposing counsel in the lobby and stop to joke with him, "Got the better of you that time," or, "Well, you were too much for me."

Meanwhile his counsel has been eloquent, in an academic way. Lomax has nothing to complain of. The opening speech for the defence. A simple defence: murder at the victim's request; a man threatened by a mortal disease. An act of friendship; an exaggerated act of friendship, it may be said; but shall it be called the less noble for that? But Lomax sees it coldly; he judges dispassionately, as though the story were not his own. Here stands this man; the jury will hear him tell how, out of compassion for a man he barely knew, he exposed himself to the utmost risk; even the precautions of common prudence were neglected by him in the urgency and delicacy of the circumstances. Another man would have refused this friendly office; or, accepting it, would have ensured his personal safety by a written assurance; or, thirdly, would have hurried from the house before the death had taken place. Not so the prisoner. Prisoner had remained for two hours with the dead body of his friend in the room, dealing with his

91

private papers according to instructions previously received. (Here the prisoner was observed to show some signs of emotion.) Again, the prisoner might have pleaded not guilty; but, regretting his inaccuracies at the time of the inquest, had refused to do so. He was determined to tell the whole truth and to throw himself upon the mercy of the jury.

Lomax realised fully the impossible task his obstinacy had imposed upon his unfortunate counsel.

He realised too, however, that the difficulties improved the game, from the point of view of his counsel. How great would his triumph be, supposing . . .! And, after all, it was nothing but a game.

"A helpless fellow," said counsel to his wife that night, over his port. "I never had to deal with such a case,—never. Of course, if I can get him off, I'm made," and he fell to ruminating, and his wife, who was in love with him, knew better than to interrupt.

How strange a colour were faces in the mass! A face examined separately and in detail was pink, porous, distinctive with mouth and eyebrows, but taken collectively they were of a uniform buff, and wore but one expression, of imbecile curiosity. Upturned, vacuous curiosity. Lomax had a prolonged opportunity for looking down upon such a mass. Here and there he picked out a face he knew,—Artivale, Robert Whitaker, the captain of the *Nereid*,—and wondered vaguely what strands had drawn them all together at that place. Only by an effort of concentration could he connect them with himself. The voice went on, telling the truth on his behalf. The jury leaned forward to stare at him. The judge, with a long face and dewlaps like a blood-hound, up under his canopy, drew pictures on his blotting-paper. Outside in the streets, sen-

93

sational posters flowered against the railings with the noonday editions. The Coati in the Zoo waggled his snout; at Mme. Tussaud's the waxen murderers stood accumulating dust in the original dock of the Old Bailey; the *Nereid*, stripped of her wings, swayed a forlorn hulk in the mud at Brightlingsea.

The prosecution was thick with argument. It bore down upon Lomax like a fog through which he could not find his way. He heard his piteous motives scouted; he heard the exquisite ridicule: he saw a smile of derision flicker across the jury. And he sympathised. He quite saw that he could not expect to be believed. If only Bellamy had not left him that fortune, he might have stood a chance. But he would not be so ungenerous as to criticise Bellamy.

That was the first day of the prosecution. Lomax at night in his cell was almost happy: he was glad to endure this for Bellamy's sake. He had loved Bellamy. He was glad

94

to know at last how much he had loved Bellamy. And his privilege had been to spare Bellamy years of intolerable life. He never stopped to argue that Bellamy might just as well have performed the function for himself; for Bellamy was a coward,—had said so once and for all, and Lomax had accepted it. Lomax did not sleep much that night, but a sort of exultation kept him going: he had saved Bellamy, Artivale would have the money, and it was still just possible that to Miss Whitaker he had rendered a service. Not much of a service, certainly, to provide her with a convicted murderer upon whom to father her child; but, between himself and his own conscience, he knew that his intentions had been honourable. His brain was perfectly clear that night. He knew that he must hold on to those three things, and he would go compensated to the scaffold.

On the second day two of his three things were taken from him.

The first was the harder to bear. Post-mortem had revealed no mortal disease in the exhumed body. Lomax, lack-lustre in the dock, stirred to brief interest: so Bellamy, too, had been of the same company? But what Bellamy had really believed would now never be known.

The second concerned Miss Whitaker. Before she was called, the court was cleared, counsel submitting that the evidence about to be produced was of too delicate and private a character for publication. Ah, thought Lomax, here is a delicacy they can understand! He sat quiet while feet shuffled out of the court, herded away by a bailiff. Then when the doors were closed he heard the now familiar voice: Evelyn Amy Whitaker.

She was in the witness-box. She was very much frightened, but she had been sub-

poenaed, and Robert had terrorised her.
She would not look at Lomax. Was she
resident at 40 College Buildings, Kensing-
ton? She was. She had known the prisoner
since April of the present year. She had
met him on Mr. Bellamy's yacht. They had
sailed from Southampton to Alexandria and
from thence had travelled by train to Cairo.
In Cairo she had married the prisoner.

Here Lomax's counsel protested that the
evidence was irrelevant.

Counsel for the Crown maintained that
the evidence was necessary to throw light
upon the prisoner's character, and the objec-
tion was overruled.

Examination continued: the marriage
took place entirely at the prisoner's suggestion. He had appeared very strange, and
insisted upon wearing coloured spectacles
even when not in the sun,—but here another
protest was raised, and allowed by his lordship. Prisoner had always been very much

97

interested in Mr. Bellamy, and occasionally said he could not understand him; also asked witness and Mr. Artivale their opinion. She had never heard Mr. Bellamy make any reference to his health. She had known Mr. Bellamy and the prisoner to be closeted for long talks in Mr. Bellamy's cabin.

Cross-examined by counsel for the defence: was it not a fact that she had led the prisoner to believe that she was with child by a man then living abroad? and that prisoner's suggestion of marriage was prompted by considerations of chivalry? Certainly not.

Dr. Edward Williams, of Harley Street, gynaecologist, examined: he had attended the witness, and could state upon oath that she was not in the condition described. The lady was, in fact, he might add, a virgin.

Lomax listened to this phantasmagoria of truth and untruth. He could have thanked the doctor for the outstanding and indubi-

table accuracy of his statement. It shone
out like a light in darkness.

His lordship, much irritated: "I cannot
have this."

As your lordship pleases.

But the jury looked paternally at Miss
Whitaker, thinking that she had had a lucky
escape.

And again Lomax sympathised with the
scepticism of the jury. Again he saw that
he could not expect to be believed. "People
don't do such things"; men were not quixotic
to that extent. Of course they could not
believe. Why, he himself, in his pre-
spectacle days, would not have believed.
He scarcely believed now. The spectacles
were really responsible; but it would only
make matters worse to tell the jury about
the spectacles. There was no place for such
things in a tribunal; and, since all life was a
tribunal, there should be no place for such
things in life. The evidence for the defence

was already sufficiently weak. Lomax had never known the name of the doctor who had given Bellamy his death-sentence, and advertisement had failed to produce him. Artivale, an impassioned witness, had had his story immediately pulled to pieces. Lomax himself was examined. But it all sounded very thin. And now that he was deprived of his spectacles,—was become again that ordinary man, that Arthur Lomax getting through existence, with only the information of that fantastic interlude, as though it concerned another man, the information rather than the memory, since it existed now for him in words and not in sensation,—now that he was returned to his pre-spectacle days, he could survey his story with cold hard sense and see that it could bear no relation to a world of fact. It was a mistake, he had always known that it was a mistake, to mix one's manners. And for having permitted himself that luxury, he was about to be hanged. It was perhaps an excessive penalty, but Lomax was not one to complain.

Miss Whitaker came to visit him in prison. She was his wife, however shamefully he had treated her, and had no difficulty in obtaining the necessary permission from compassionate authority. Lomax was pleased to see her. She reminded him of Illyria and the Coati,—though, of course, Illyria and the Coati were things he knew of only by hearsay. But Miss Whitaker herself was a little embarrassed; was almost sorry she had come. Like Lomax, she found reality confusing. "I am afraid you have ruined your life," she said, looking round Lomax's neat cell.

"Not at all," said Lomax politely, "so long as I haven't ruined yours. I am only sorry my counsel should have mentioned that about the child. He got it out of me in an unguarded moment. I am glad to have this opportunity of apologising."

"Yes, poor little thing," said Miss Whitaker. "But as my name hasn't appeared, no harm was done. I was sorry, too, that I had to give evidence against you. Robert insisted,—I always warned you that Robert was very revengeful."

"Quite," said Lomax.

"I ought to tell you," said Miss Whitaker, looking down at her shoes, "that *he* is coming home. He has been among the Indians for the last six months, and it has broken his health. He lands at Southampton,—where we sailed from, do you remember?—just before Christmas."

"I am sorry," said Lomax, "that I shan't have the pleasure of meeting him."

"No," said Miss Whitaker; and then, seeming to lose her head a little, she again said, "No; of course you won't. Perhaps I ought to be going?"

Anyway, Artivale would have the money. Lomax hugged that to his breast. Science would have the money; and science was a fact, surely, incapable of caricature; absolute, as mathematics were absolute. He had had enough of living in a world where truth was falsehood and falsehood truth. He was about to abandon that world, and his only legacy to it should be to an incorruptible province; let him hold that comfort, where all other comforts had turned to so ingenious a mockery.

Shortly after Lomax had been hanged, Bellamy's nearest relations, two maiden ladies who lived at Hampstead and interested themselves in the conversion of the heathen, entered a plea that Bellamy's will had been composed under the undue influence of Arthur Lomax. The case was easily proved, and it was understood that the bulk of the fortune would be placed by the next-of-kin as conscience money at the disposal of His Majesty's Treasury.